Flaggin' the Dragon

Grandma Light

AuthorHouse™ UK Ltd.
500 Avebury Boulevard
Central Milton Keynes, MK9 2BE
www.authorhouse.co.uk
Phone: 08001974150

First published by AuthorHouse 6/17/2009

ISBN: 978-1-4389-9105-4 (sc)

Printed in the United States of America
Bloomington, Indiana

This book is printed on acid-free paper.

authorHOUSE®

Dedicated to my Granddaughter Samantha

On her Seventh Birthday
January 9, 2007

Once there was a Dragon
Who decided he wanted a wagon
To keep his tail from draggin'!
His name was Flaggin'.

Off went Flaggin'
To find his little wagon
His spirits, they were saggin'
'Cause his tail was draggin'.

He came upon a Tree Stump
To ask about a wagon.
The Stump was stumped and in quite a slump
And could not help out Flaggin'.

He came upon a River
"Have you seen a wagon?"
The River gave a shiver.
It had never seen a wagon.
Poor Flaggin'. His tail was draggin'.

A bright Blue Jay flew down, as if to say, "Hey"
"Have you seen a wagon to keep my tail
from draggin'?"
"Hey, Hey," said the Jay, "Seen none today!
Gotta go. Gotta play.
Can't stay. Can't stay."
Poor Flaggin'. His tail was still draggin'.

Gray Squirrel, "Have you seen a wagon
To keep my tail from draggin'?
Gray Squirrel was busy burying a nut.
He scampered here and he scampered there
Gathering food for the winter.
"What would I know about a wagon?"
My tail's never draggin'!

Just then Flaggin' saw Chipper the Chipmunk
And said, "Chipper, have you seen a wagon
To keep my tail from draggin'?

Chipper with his cheeks full of nuts stuttered,
"Why, no little friend,
I have never seen a wagon.
What's a wagon?"

Merry Merry Mushroom.
Mushroom in the moss!
"Have you seen a wagon
to keep my tail from draggin'?"
Merry Mushroom replied,
Because she was wise.
"Perhaps you should see
the Golden Fairy in the Forrest,
She knows everything."

Yippee! Flaggin' felt happy. Which way?
"Follow your heart," Merry Mushroom smiled.
"How will I know?"
"Your heart will tell you."
Merry Mushroom's voice faded in the distance.

Soon Flaggin' became tired
And fell asleep in the middle of a ring of yellow daisies.
A Golden Fairy appeared to him in a dream.
She said, "Fly Flaggin,' Then your tail won't be draggin'."

When he awakened he looked at her
Reflection in a crystal clear brook,
And to his surprise, he saw himself.
He had wings
Every color of the Rainbow.

He remembered he could fly!

Off Flaggin' flew – his tail no longer draggin'.
He didn't need a wagon!
The skies were laughing, and his
Papa was braggin'.

Flaggin' outgrew his need for a wagon.
Now his tail was waggin'.
'Cause it was no longer draggin'.
Flaggin' was a flying Dragon.

And that boys and girls is the
Story of how a Dragonfly came to be...

Printed in the United States
153298LV00003B